The Bears' House is a very special place . . .

I don't do anything right or wrong in school, so why should Miss Thompson notice me? I'm not dumb and I'm not smart. I never raise my hand to answer, but sometimes when she calls on me, I know the answer. And I don't whisper or pass notes. Who to? Only time I want her to notice me is when I finish my math ahead of everybody else and bring the paper to her.

"All right, Fran Ellen," she will say. "You may play with the Bears' House."

And then I'm there, in the back of the room. And I settle down on the chair in front of the Bears' House, and I get my thumb in my mouth, and forget all about Jennifer James and Susan Rogers, and everything else . . .

"What kind of a children's book is this? The best that Marilyn Sachs has written. . . . It is a shattering, a tragic book—tragic in the very truth of its picture of the need to love and be loved in return."

—*The New York Times Book Review*

THE BEARS' HOUSE

PUFFIN BOOKS BY MARILYN SACHS

At the Sound of the Beep
The Bears' House
Circles
Class Pictures
Peter and Veronica
A Pocket Full of Seeds
Thirteen Going on Seven
The Truth about Mary Rose
Veronica Ganz
What My Sister Remembered

THE BEARS' HOUSE

MARILYN SACHS

PUFFIN BOOKS

PUFFIN BOOKS
Published by the Penguin Group
Penguin Books USA Inc., 375 Hudson Street, New York, New York 10014, U.S.A.
Penguin Books Ltd, 27 Wrights Lane, London W8 5TZ, England
Penguin Books Australia Ltd, Ringwood, Victoria, Australia
Penguin Books Canada Ltd, 10 Alcorn Avenue, Toronto, Ontario, Canada M4V 3B2
Penguin Books (N.Z.) Ltd, 182-190 Wairau Road, Auckland 10, New Zealand
Penguin Books Ltd, Registered Offices: Harmondsworth, Middlesex, England

The Bears' House was first published in 1971 by Doubleday & Company, Inc.,
  with illustrations by Louis Glanzman
Published by E. P. Dutton, 1987
Published in Puffin Books, 1996

10 9 8 7 6 5 4 3

THE LIBRARY OF CONGRESS HAS CATALOGED THE DUTTON EDITION AS FOLLOWS:
Sachs, Marilyn.
The bears' house.
Summary: Although she sucks her thumb, smells bad, and loses herself in the
make-believe world of the three bears' dollhouse, ten-year-old Fran knows
how to take care of her baby sister better than anybody else.
[1. Family problems—Fiction. 2. Teachers—Fiction.
3. Schools—Fiction.] I. Title.
PZ7.S1187B 1987 [Fic] 86-29267
ISBN 0-525-44286-3

Puffin ISBN 0-14-038321-2

Printed in the United States of America

With love to the grandmas—

Sarah
So So
and
Nellie

JANUARY

Everybody in my class knows my name.

It's Fran Ellen Smith. I'm nearly ten. I suck my thumb, and everybody says I smell bad. (I can smell my smell. It's a sucking smell. I don't think it's bad. It smells like me.)

Everybody knows my name. I don't care if they do. But nobody knows about me and the Bears' House. Nobody ever will.

The Bears' House is up on a table at the back of my classroom. Teacher's father made it for her when she was a little girl, long, long ago. That's Miss Thompson. Only she was called Blanche then. She didn't look like she looks now. I know because inside the house there is a fireplace, and right over the fireplace, there is a tiny picture of a girl with long curls. The picture has a fancy gold frame, a teeny-tiny one, and underneath it is like a metal

1

plate that teacher calls a plaque. The plaque says BLANCHE'S HOUSE, and the picture is Blanche, and that was Miss Thompson when she was little.

Only it's not Blanche's house any more. It's my house. My picture should be hanging over the fireplace, and the plaque should say FRAN ELLEN'S HOUSE. The three bears live in the house, so it's their house too. My house and their house. Nobody else's.

Right now, they're outside the house, coming up the stairs, three china dolls with brown bears' hair and big smiles on their faces. But they won't keep on smiling when they find Goldilocks in their baby's bed.

Because she's there—asleep—a little, hard, white doll with hard, yellow painted hair, and little blue eyes that open and close. But now they're closed because she's asleep in Baby Bear's bed.

Everything in that house was made by Miss Thompson's father or mother except Goldilocks and the three bears. In those days, Miss Thompson says, mothers and fathers took good care of their children, and children were respectful and clean. Miss Thompson is always talking about other times when people were better and always respectful and clean, especially around teachers.

She's been teaching at P.S. 87 for more than thirty years, she says, and even the children years ago were better than they are today. Everything was better, and she ought to know.

I can tell it was better because of the Bears' House. If children had fathers who made them presents like that, it must have been better.

The house has three rooms, and is all open in the back. Downstairs there is the kitchen, and the living room, and upstairs, a great big bedroom.

The front door has a knocker on the outside, and a itty-bitty floor mat in front of it that says WEL-COME. All the windows have glass, and open and shut. Miss Thompson says that never once has the glass broken in any one of those windows. She says it's because her father did such a great job, putting the glass in and joining all the parts that got joined. That's why, she says, in all the thirty years the Bears' House has been sitting in P.S. 87, and has been played with by all those kids, not one single piece of glass ever cracked.

Maybe, like she says, it was because her father knew what he was doing, but I think it must have been that all those kids made sure not to break the windows. I think maybe all those kids must have loved the Bears' House, only none of them ever loved it the way I do.

I don't even have to touch it any more. I did, in the beginning. But now I know without looking that if you open the closet upstairs in the bedroom, there are five dresses hanging on little hangers that are for Mama Bear. One of them is made out of blue satin, with pearls around the neck. That one is a ball gown, teacher said. Not to wear to ball games, like Henry Jackson thought, but to big, fancy dances that people use to call balls. The blue satin dress is real pretty, but Mama Bear has a bright yellow and red flowered dress with all kinds of ruffles, and a straw hat with red ribbons, and lots of flowers to match. I like that one the best.

All the beds have sheets on them, and pillow cases with lace on the edges. Baby Bear's bed is like a crib, and his blanket is made of pieces of material Miss Thompson calls a patchwork quilt.

Miss Thompson lets some children help her take care of the house. The children who are best behaved in December get to help in the New Year Cleaning in January. I didn't get picked. Jennifer James did, and Carol Moreno and Franklin Coates. They washed the windows and waxed the floors and polished the furniture. Teacher told them to take the pictures off the walls, and wipe the dust off them. One of the pictures, Miss Thompson says *she* made after she got the house. It's embroidery, and it says GOD BLESS THIS HOUSE.

I guess I am lucky. I am lucky to have Miss Thompson for my teacher. If I was a year younger or got left back, I would not be in this fourth-grade class now, and I would not have Miss Thompson. If there was no Miss Thompson, there would be no Bears' House.

"Where you going, teacher, after this term?" somebody will ask.

"I am retiring," says Miss Thompson, and talks about all those thirty years, and how she's getting too old and tired.

"Who's getting the Bears' House, teacher?"

"I still have not decided," says Miss Thompson, "but as I told you at the beginning of this year, the child who *earns* it, the child who most deserves it, the child who works the hardest to improve himself and demonstrates . . ."

That's the way she talks—on and on, with words that don't mean anything.

And then Jennifer James and Rosalie Gonzales kind of eye one another up and down. Everybody knows it's got to be one or the other of them. Rosalie's the smartest kid in the class, and she keeps bringing those fat books into school to show teacher what she's reading. But Jennifer is teacher's pet, and she's always running errands for Miss Thompson and laughing and snuggling up to her. You can see Miss Thompson can't help herself liking Jennifer best. So I think Jennifer will get it. And that's the way it should be. If you have something precious, and you're going to give it away, if it was me, I'd give it to someone I liked most—like my baby sister Flora.

So that's why I am lucky to be in Miss Thompson's class this year. Next year there won't be any Miss Thompson, and there won't be any Bears' House. I don't like to think about next year. Because, like I told you, it is really my house, and it will go right on being my house whoever she gives it to.

Every day I try to be with the Bears' House. Any kid who finishes first in reading or math can play with the Bears' House until the rest of the class catches up. I never finish first in reading but lots of times I do in math. That's because I take the book home the night before, and do the work at home. After Flora's asleep I got lots of time.

"All right, Fran Ellen, you may play with the Bears' House," Miss Thompson will say.

And I'll walk over real slow, and act kind of like it's no big deal playing with the Bears' House. I am very careful because I think if she knew what really was happening, she would not let me play with it.

So I get myself back there, and I settle myself down in front of it, and get my thumb in my mouth, and get ready. Like I said, I never touch it. I don't have to touch it.

Sometimes Miss Thompson will say after awhile,

"Fran Ellen, you can handle anything you like if you are careful."

And once she said, "I wonder why you even bother going over to the Bears' House. You only sit there with your thumb in your mouth. I don't think you even know the Bears' House is there."

"Yes, ma'am," I say to her.

And I open the door, and walk in.

fEbRUARY

I have another house besides the Bears' House. It's where I live with my family. It doesn't look anything like the Bears' House. It never looked like the Bears' House, but before Mama got sick it looked a lot better than it does now.

Everything looked better then. Except for Flora. She gets more beautiful every day. I guess she must be the most beautiful baby in the whole world. And it's not because she's my sister, because I don't feel that way about my other sisters. One of my sisters I even hate.

There are four girls in my family and one boy. All of us have names that start with F. Fletcher is the oldest. He's twelve and a half, and pretty smart and not usually mean. Next comes Florence. She's eleven and mean. She's the one I hate—most of the time. Then there's me, and I already told you about

8

me. Next comes Felice who's five. She's fat, and spits when she talks. I don't care for her so much, but I don't hate her the way I do Florence. And last is Flora, my beautiful baby, Flora, and she's seven months.

My daddy and mama have names that start with F too. Mama's name is Francine and Daddy's name is Fred—Frederick—Frederick Emerson. Everybody's got a middle name in my family—Fletcher Thurman, Florence Anne, Felice Georgene, Flora Elizabeth and Mama is Francine Norma. But I'm the only one who gets called by both my names. Maybe it's because everything I do is different from everybody else. So even what I get called has to be different.

My daddy doesn't live with us any more. Nobody knows where he is. One day he just wasn't here. Mama thought he went back to Harlan. That's in Alabama. To see Uncle Wilt. We come from Harlan. My daddy and his daddy and Uncle Wilt used to have a service station and garage in Harlan. Then my granddaddy died, and Daddy and Uncle Wilt started arguing all the time. So Uncle Wilt gave my daddy some money, and we moved up North three years ago. But Daddy always said Uncle Wilt cheated him. Especially when we didn't have any more money left, and Mama had to give up her job.

It was a nice job. She worked in a bakery store that sold doughnuts, and every night she brought home a big bag full of different kinds of doughnuts. She used to wear a white dress to work, and she looked like a nurse, and smelled like powdered sugar.

Then Flora was born, and Mama had some trouble. The doctor said she had to stay home for a while. That's when we went on welfare. Daddy was not happy when Flora was born. Who needed another girl, he said. Four daughters was four too many mouths to feed. Daddy never could find a steady job up here, and he started talking all the time about how Uncle Wilt cheated him out of his share of the business, and how he was going back to Harlan to have it out with him.

So when he didn't come home, Mama said he must have gone back to Harlan. She even wrote to Uncle Wilt. We didn't hear anything so she wrote again. Then Uncle Wilt wrote back and said Daddy never came, and he didn't think he would come. Uncle Wilt said he had no more money to spare, and that Mama shouldn't bother writing him any more letters. If Daddy did show up, he'd tell him to write.

That's when Mama started crying. She couldn't even take care of Flora any more. And like I told you, there's just no baby in this whole world like Flora. She's not only beautiful, she's good, better than good. She's perfect. All day long she sleeps or sings or laughs. She never cries. Isn't that funny?

She never cries, but Mama cries all the time. Cries and sleeps.

That's all she does now. Except sometimes she goes and looks in the mailbox. It used to be Mama always had something good cooking on the stove—chicken or beans or pie. Mama always talked a lot, and smacked a lot too. If we didn't wash up and change our underwear and shine our shoes—watch out! She used to sweep up every day, and wash the floors twice a week, and put down wax. Now she doesn't care.

"Mama, Felice knocked the catchup on the floor, and there's glass all over, and she won't pick it up. Mama!"

Nothing. She just cries and sleeps.

She didn't get like that all at once. It came on gradual, but one day, Fletcher told us she couldn't take care of us any more. Fletcher said there were three things we could do:

1) We could write Uncle Wilt and tell him Daddy never came back, Mama was sick and we didn't have anybody looking after us. Probably, Fletcher said, Uncle Wilt would make us all come back to Harlan and live with him.

Nobody liked that idea. Uncle Wilt is mean. He and Aunt Janine don't have any children, and don't like children, especially us. They have a little house that is filled up with things that children can't touch.

There is no room for anybody else in that house besides Uncle Wilt, Aunt Janine and their things.

2) Nobody is very friendly in this building, but Fletcher said we could tell one of the neighbors what was happening. Fletcher said he guessed that person would probably call the police, and they would come and put Mama away in a hospital for crazy people and take us to foster homes. Probably, Fletcher said, we wouldn't be together, and maybe we would never see each other again for the rest of our lives.

That's when Felice started howling, and Florence started howling, and I guess I wasn't so quiet either. Not that I'd mind so much never seeing Florence again or even Felice. I guess I would miss Fletcher though—and Mama—the way she used to be. But it was Flora that really shook me. Thinking about them coming and taking Flora away from me. I knew right off I wasn't going to let anybody take Flora away from me.

Well then, Fletcher said, if we didn't like his first two suggestions, maybe we'd prefer his third. And this was it:

3) We don't tell anybody anything. We don't say anything about Daddy, and especially, we don't say anything about Mama. Fletcher said it won't be long before Mama is all well again, and then things will go on the way they always did. But in the meantime,

everybody's got to shut up. He looked at Felice when he said that. She's only five, and a blabbermouth.

"I won't tell. I won't tell," she began yelling.

"Or they'll come and put you away in jail," said Florence, "and never give you any cookies, and pinch you all the time if you cry . . ."

Felice got the message, and we all agreed that we liked his third idea the best. O.K., said Fletcher, but we were going to need a system so that nobody would find out. Since he was the oldest, said Fletcher, and the man of the house, he would handle the money. He would do all the shopping, pay the bills, write letters, and do all the talking to grownups. We could only say "Hello," "Good-by" and "Fine" if anybody asked us how we were. All the other talking he would do. And that included the Welfare Lady too. Fletcher said he would also take care of Mama.

Which was only right. Mama always liked Fletcher the best. She was always so proud of him. When my daddy used to fuss about how Fletcher was a sissy because he read books all the time . . . and wasn't no good at sports . . . and cried if someone hit him, Mama always stuck up for Fletcher. She said he'd be something special one of these days. And even now, if anybody can get her to feel better, it's still him. Some days if we offer her something to eat, she just won't. But then Fletcher will come inside her room, and say, "Come on now, Mama, that's a good girl," and she'll eat and drink for him just the way Flora does for me.

Fletcher is the only one who can get Mama up when the Welfare Lady comes around snooping. He gets Mama to stop crying, and even answer the lady's questions. Sometimes the lady talks to us, and asks us how we all are, and do we have enough to eat, and are we comfortable.

Then Fletcher starts smiling, and we smile too, but he does all the talking. "Yes, ma'am," Fletcher will say, "we just couldn't be better." And maybe he'll talk about the baby and get her looking at the baby. Nobody can help feeling good when they look at my baby.

I keep the baby nice. But sometimes I don't get to pick up around the house, and if Fletcher sees the Welfare Lady looking at the floor or the dishes in the sink, he gets after us later. And then Florence yells at me and kicks me and pinches me. Once she even bit me on my shoulder. The bite marks are still there.

Because she says I'm supposed to clean the house. She says she's supposed to take care of the baby, and I'm supposed to take care of the house. Which is a laugh because Florence doesn't do anything around here except complain, or be mean.

14

But that time I was telling you about, when Fletcher was explaining about his system, he said Florence and me would have to take care of the house and look after Flora.

Florence said O.K., she'd take care of the baby and do the cooking, and that I should clean the house.

"No," I said. "I'll take care of the baby and do the cooking, and you clean the house."

That's when Florence bit me on the shoulder. After she pulled my hair and smacked my face.

Right away I stuck my thumb in my mouth and shouted, "Who you hitting?"

Then Felice began smacking me too.

I don't know why I keep doing it, and I wish I could stop, but I can't. Whenever anybody hits me, I always say, "Who you hitting?" I don't hit back, but I get my thumb in my mouth and I say it. Then everybody else around piles on too. It makes people mad when I say, "Who you hitting?" I know it makes them mad, and I tell myself, before anyone hits me, when I see them coming for me, I say O.K., you're going to get it again but just don't go making it worse by sucking your thumb and saying, "Who you hitting?" Maybe you could even try hitting back.

But I never do hit back. And I always do suck my

thumb and say, "Who you hitting?" soon as someone pokes me.

Only Fletcher doesn't hit me. He made Florence and Felice stop that time. But he didn't look at me like he liked what he was looking at.

"Florence will take care of the baby and do the cooking," said Fletcher. "You, Fran Ellen, will do the cleaning."

So you know what? I clean the house *and* take care of the baby, and Florence doesn't do anything. There's no cooking to do because Fletcher does the shopping and most of the time it's canned spaghetti or ravioli or pork and beans. Good things, but all Florence has to do is heat them up, and sometimes we're too hungry to wait so she doesn't even have to do that. For dessert we have either chocolate doughnuts or chocolate grahams. The food is pretty good, except sometimes I remember how my daddy used to take us out for pizza, and I miss that.

Breakfast we all have Sugar Pops or Cocoa Crispies. I don't know what Felice has for lunch, but she's fat and always eating, so we don't have to worry about her. Us three older ones eat the free hot lunches in school. I have to eat fast so I can run home to feed the baby. Florence is supposed to do it, but she doesn't. She is also supposed to get up earlier in the morning to fix the baby's breakfast and change her, but she doesn't do that either.

And I'm glad she doesn't. Because I love Flora best in the whole world, and she loves me best. She doesn't want anybody else but me to take care of her. And I won't let anybody else take care of her. Nobody knows how, except me. That's why Flora is so beautiful and so happy. Because I take care of her. I guess I am lucky that Florence is lazy.

So I run home at lunchtime. Felice goes to afternoon kindergarten, and she's home mornings. Most of the time, the baby will sleep all morning, but if she fusses, Felice can give her a bottle of Kool-Aid. It's the afternoons I worry about. Because Felice is in school, and the baby is alone—not counting Mama —for over two hours. Lately, I been sneaking home during afternoon recess.

Miss Thompson never caught me. She never notices me except when I'm around. When I'm gone, nobody notices me.

MARCH

Recess is the worst. Like I told you, *now* I run home at lunchtime, but even before I used to run home lunchtime was never as bad as recess. Because after we finished eating, and they made us go out in the yard, there were so many kids I could get lost someplace where nobody noticed me. Sometimes I could even stay in one of the toilets, and sit on the seat and just relax, suck my thumb and get real comfortable.

But recess comes after you go to the toilet—once in the morning and once in the afternoon. When you go out in the yard at recess you have to stay with your class. Afternoon recess I go home. I wait until the whole class goes out in the yard, and when the line breaks, just before they choose up for kickball or four square, I slide around the side of the building, go back inside through one of the side doors, down the stairs, and out through the back basement door. Nobody ever noticed I was gone.

But morning recess, there's always somebody notices me. Like maybe I try not to play, and go stand near the drinking fountain. Miss Thompson will come over and say, "Why are you standing over here, Fran Ellen?"

"I'm taking a drink, ma'am," I say.

"I don't see how you can take a drink and go on sucking your thumb, Fran Ellen."

"Yes, ma'am."

"And take your thumb out of your mouth when you speak to me. A big girl your age has no business sucking her thumb."

"Yes, ma'am."

"Yes, ma'am what? Don't you ever say anything else besides 'Yes, ma'am'?"

"No, ma'am."

Something like that. So she'll make me go back, and I'll get to be picked last for the team unless Georgie Cooper is in school that day. He's a mental, and the kids hate him more than me, except they don't tangle with him anymore. Because he's wild, and one day when Brian Jamison said he had cooties, Georgie put his hands around Brian's neck and squeezed. It took two teachers, Miss Thompson and Mrs. Feinstein, to pull him off, and Brian's eyes looked like they were going to pop out. So nobody

19

notices Georgie Cooper, but they pick him last for teams.

So then, when it's my turn up, if I miss the ball, somebody like Jennifer James will give me a kick as I go by. And if I'm on the field and don't catch a ball—and it's hard to catch balls when you keep one finger in your mouth, so I don't know why they make me play—a couple of them will call me "Thumb Sucker." Only it sounds worse than that. When the game's over, even if we won, somebody's sure to notice I didn't play right and poke me in the stomach.

There is a game Jennifer and Susan Rogers like to play, and every day during recess, if I'm on their team, and we're all waiting for our turns, that's the time they play it. I kind of expect it every day, and the funny thing is if it doesn't happen, I'm happy but I feel like something was missing that day. This is how they play the game.

"Call Susan a dope," Jennifer will say to me.

Susan is the biggest kid in the class and hits the hardest. So naturally, I stick my thumb in my mouth, and shake my head No.

Then they both nudge each other and point at me and say, "Look at the baby" or "Thumb Sucker" or "Yuk!" Something like that, and they say how much I smell. Then, after awhile, Jennifer says again,

"Go ahead, Fran Ellen, call Susan a dope. Honest, she won't mind. Right, Susan?"

Susan smiles her mean, snake smile, and says, "Sure, I won't get mad."

"Go ahead now, Fran Ellen."

"Uh, uh," I say, and keep my thumb nice and wet between my lips.

Jennifer James is pretty. She's pretty mean too, but she's pretty. She's got dimples, and cool clothes, and she's teacher's pet. She's got different colored tights and about five pairs of shoes. They're all pretty, but I like the orange patent leather ones the best. So that day, maybe she'll be wearing the orange leather shoes, and she'll step hard on my foot with her pretty orange patent leather shoes and say in a friendly voice, "Ooh, excuse me, Fran Ellen, but I really think you should call Susan a dope. Go ahead, call her a dope, and she won't do anything."

You get the idea, and after awhile I do call Susan a dope, and Susan will smack me in the face, and Jennifer will kick me, and anybody else who has a hand or foot free is welcome to join in. Meantime, I'll be keeping my finger safe in my mouth, and crying, "Who you hitting?"

Sometimes Miss Thompson will come over and stop it, and ask what happened.

"She called me a dope, Miss Thompson," Susan

will say like her feelings are real hurt. "I didn't do nothing to her, Miss Thompson, and she said I was a dope, and my mother was a dope. (Sometimes they make me say Susan's mother was a dope too.) And nobody's going to call my mother a dope."

You can see Miss Thompson thinks nobody should let anybody call her mother a dope. But she asks me is it true—did I call Susan a dope, or Susan's mother a dope, or maybe even Susan's sister, Josie, a dope. I have to say Yes. So then she tells Susan she must not hit anyone, but to come and tell her, Miss Thompson, if anybody insults any member of her family, and she will promise to take care of it.

Then she turns to me. "Come with me, Fran Ellen," she says, and takes me off for a private talk.

"Stand over there," she says because she doesn't care to have me and my smell too close. She says, "Why is it, Fran Ellen, you always have to be insulting people? I can't blame Susan for being angry, and I can't understand why you continually pick on her. And take that thumb out of your mouth!"

And so on and so on. But most of the time, Susan and Jennifer try to play their game when teacher isn't looking.

If it wasn't for them, Miss Thompson wouldn't notice me so much. I don't do anything right or wrong in school, so why should she notice me. I'm not dumb and I'm not smart. I never raise my hand to answer, but sometimes when she calls on me, I know the answer. And I don't whisper or pass notes. Who to? Only time I want her to notice me is when I finish my math ahead of everybody else and bring the paper to her.

"All right, Fran Ellen," she will say. "You may play with the Bears' House."

And then I'm there, in the back of the room. And I settle down on the chair in front of the Bears' House, and I get my thumb in my mouth, and forget all about Jennifer James and Susan Rogers, and everything else. I feel good.

I feel good with Flora, my baby, too—only it's different. When I take care of Flora, it's the only time I'm not sucking my thumb, and that's O.K. Only it's not me. But I'm me in the Bears' House.

The door is open, naturally, and I go up the stairs and stand by the bed. She opens her eyes.

"Move over!" I tell her, and she says, "Yes, ma'am."

"You sure are some pushy, good-for-nothing," I tell her. "What kind of nerve you got, anyway, pushing yourself in here where you weren't invited and eating up a family's food and breaking their furniture and messing up their beds!"

"Yes, ma'am," says Goldilocks. She gets out of the bed, and I get in. But I go on telling her what I

23

think of her, and all she can say is, "Yes, ma'am," and suck her thumb.

"Thumb Sucker," I tell her.

Then we both suck our thumbs together for a while, and I get over being mad at her.

Later when the bears get home, I tell her she better go.

"Where should I go?" she says, and starts crying. The tears go rolling down her face. They are see-through tears, and you can see those red cheeks of hers through them.

"O.K.," I tell her. "Stop making all that racket. You got yourself into this mess, but I will see what I can do for you. Wait here!"

So she hides under the bed, and I go marching down the stairs. There's real carpet on the stairs, and they don't hear me.

The three of them are in the living room. Papa Bear is looking at his chair. It's a great big chair with red cushions. The seat cushion is all pressed down, and he says, "Who's been sitting in my chair?"

Mama Bear doesn't even bother to answer him. She's looking at her chair. It's a rocking chair with light blue cushions. There's a foot mark on one of the cushions. Mama Bear's good and mad—the way my mama used to be when we put our feet on the furniture.

"Somebody's been sitting in my chair," she says, and it's a good thing Goldilocks is upstairs under the bed.

Then Baby Bear speaks up. He's cute for a bear, only he's not really a baby the way Flora is. He can talk and eat by himself. He's got a cute little chair with red and blue flowers painted over it. No cushions, but he doesn't mind because his daddy made it for him. But now, one of the legs is off, and it's leaning over in a crazy way. So naturally he's crying. He says, "Somebody's been sitting in my chair and has broken it to pieces." And then he really begins bawling.

That's when I come in. I walk into the room, and I tell them right off, "You should have your heads examined! How come you go off like that and don't lock up the door? What do you expect's going to happen if you leave the door open? Anybody can just walk in and steal everything you got. Somebody better set you straight, or one day you'll come home and there won't be nothing left."

"Who are you?" says Mama Bear. She's not smiling, but you can see she kind of admires me.

"I'm Fran Ellen Smith," I tell her, "and I like you very much, and I like your family very much, and your house very much. You keep it real nice, and I'm glad to meet you, but I think you should lock up when you go out."

25

"You're right!" Mama Bear smiles and says, "I'm glad to meet you too. Won't you sit down, and have a bite to eat?"

"Thank you, Mama Bear," I say, and we all go into the kitchen, and sit around the table that has a red-and-white tablecloth on it. Mama Bear opens the icebox. They didn't have refrigerators then. You should just see what's inside. Three pies—one's lemon, one's apple and one's cherry. There's a turkey, and a big cheese, and a strawberry cake, and butter, and a pitcher of cream and roast beef, and corn on the cob and pancakes. That's only for a start. But one thing there isn't, and that's porridge. She never has any porridge, and I always mean to ask her how come, but I keep forgetting. Maybe next time.

Then she goes and gets the dishes. They're kept in a cupboard right next to the icebox. That cupboard is cool. The top of it has glass doors, and Mama Bear opens the doors and brings out the fancy company dishes. They're white with blue flowers around the outsides. She also brings out the company glasses. The dishes are real dishes, and the glasses are real glasses. They are very special, and Mama Bear only uses them when I come.

Like that TV commercial about how your dishes shine if you use the right kind of soap, Mama Bear's dishes shine like that. I look in my plate, and there's my face, bright and shiny, smack in the middle, and the flowers look like a big, fat crown on my head.

I get a taste of everything, but mostly I concentrate on the turkey and the lemon pie.

We talk and talk and have a lot of laughs. You can see they just can't get enough of me.

Papa Bear says, "One thing I always wanted was a daughter." He looks right at me when he says it, and I kind of giggle and look away.

"Yes," he says, "and I tell you what, Fran Ellen, I'd like for you to be my daughter."

Well, I got my thumb in my mouth by this time, but nobody seems to mind about that. Nobody says anything about smells either. Papa Bear kind of picks me up and sets me in his lap, and I lean against his shoulder and don't want to go no place.

"So I tell you what, Fran Ellen," he says. "You're going to be my daughter, and I'm never going away from here."

"That's right," Mama Bear says, "nobody's going away from here. This will be Fran Ellen's house forever and ever."

Then I remember Goldilocks hiding upstairs under Papa Bear's bed. I tell them about her, but they say that's fine. I can always have a friend over. Any time.

Mama Bear and I go upstairs. Goldilocks comes out from under the bed. She's shaking all over. Her

27

thumb's in her mouth, and those little see-through tears are pouring down her cheeks.

Mama Bear says, "Now, now, child, you don't have to be afraid of me." She gives Goldilocks a kiss and Goldilocks stops crying. Then Mama Bear kisses me, and I kiss her back. She kisses me a couple more times, and she gives me a tight, squeezy hug. She's just crazy about me. I guess she just can't help herself.

She gives Goldilocks the blue satin ball gown to wear, and she tells her to stay for a nice, long visit. And me, I get the yellow and red flowered dress with the matching straw hat.

"For the fourth time, Fran Ellen, you may go back to your seat. The whole class is waiting for you."

"Yes, ma'am," I say to her.

"'Bye," I say to them. "Don't forget to lock up when you go out, and I'll be back soon as I can."

"Hurry!" they say to me.

April

I don't know why, but that day I felt scared. As soon as I snuck back into the building at recess, my feet began shaking so, I didn't see how I'd ever get myself home. I shouldn't have gone, but I got to thinking about Flora. I got to thinking maybe she was up and crying for me, even though I told you she hardly ever cries.

I went on down the stairs through the basement and out the back door. I could hardly get my feet moving. And then I thought I heard somebody else behind me. Quick, I swung around. Nobody there, but that scared feeling got inside my mouth and made my teeth rattle. Then I ran. My feet didn't shake so hard when I ran, but I started crying, and I couldn't stop. And the funny thing was, there was nothing to cry about—then. My house is around the corner from school and down half a block. By the time I got up the stairs, I was crying so hard I had to sit down just to breathe.

I didn't want to go inside. I was so scared. I sat there and I didn't know what to do. I didn't even know what I was scared of. I just sat there outside my door, and that scared feeling didn't miss one single part of me.

"Flora," I said out loud. Saying it made me feel better, so I said it a few more times. Then I jumped up, put the key in the lock and turned it twice. I ran into our bedroom where Flora's crib is, and there she was.

My baby! My Flora! She was playing with her plastic cups, and she was singing. I picked her up, and kissed her all over. I couldn't stop kissing her. She smelled good, and she smelled like she needed a change. While I changed her, she wrinkled up her nose and said, "Fra Fra." I swear she said "Fra Fra." This isn't the first time. It's me. She's saying me, Fran Ellen. I'm "Fra Fra."

I carry her into the kitchen. I love to carry her. She's not a big baby. I guess she's kind of little, but she snuggles up so nice to you. When I'm home, I carry her around a lot when she's not asleep. Maybe that's why I don't get to do the cleaning as good as I should.

The kitchen sure is a mess. Today I better clean up the dishes. That pot we heated up the ravioli in on Tuesday is still sitting on the stove, and so's the pot from Wednesday with the corned beef hash, and last night's franks and beans. That Felice went and knocked over her milk again and didn't bother to clean up. The slob!

Flora's head is on my neck. I fix her a bottle of Kool-Aid, and look around for a cookie. It's hard to keep cookies around the house without Felice eating them all up. Especially mornings when we're not home, she can knock off a whole bag.

I find a couple of Fig Newtons and go back to Flora's crib. I lay her down and watch her sucking away at her bottle and laughing up at me at the same time. Then I put the Fig Newtons down next to her and figure I better get back to school.

But first I take a look in Mama's room. I don't have to. Like I said, Fletcher looks after Mama. But sometimes I think maybe there's something I can do to make her feel better.

Mama's not sleeping. She's in bed with her eyes open, but she's not crying.

"Hello, Mama," I say. "I'm home."

Mama just looks at me. The shades are down, and it's too hot in the room. It really doesn't smell good either, and I'm not fussy about smells.

"Mama," I say, "you want something before I go back to school?"

Mama says, "Is there any mail today?"

"No, Mama," I say. "There's no mail."

"Did you look?" she says.

"Yes, Mama."

She begins to cry, and I say, "Never mind, Mama, can I fix you a glass of Kool-Aid?"

But she keeps on crying, and turns away from me. So I close the door and take a quick peek at Flora. She's singing a sleepy song, so I know she'll be napping soon. There's nothing to stop me, and I don't have that scared feeling any more, but something tells me to stay home. I should have stayed home.

Because the class is already in the classroom when I get back. That's not such a big deal because it's happened before, and I can always say I stopped off to go to the toilet. But as soon as I step into that room, I see them all looking at me, and I know I should have stayed home.

"Where have you been, Fran Ellen?" says Miss Thompson.

"In the toilet, Miss Thompson."

They all laugh, and Miss Thompson says, "All this time?"

"Yes, ma'am."

"No, you have not been, Fran Ellen. Please stay in this afternoon, and we will discuss it further."

"Yes, ma'am."

So I stay after everybody goes home, and she

says somebody saw me leave today, and somebody else said I leave lots of times, and the question is where do I go.

"To the toilet," I say.

Miss Thompson starts writing on a paper. She writes a note, and then folds it up and puts it in an envelope.

"Fran Ellen, you are to give this to your mother. I want her to come to school, and see me."

"She can't, Miss Thompson," I say, getting scared again.

"Why not?"

"Because she's sick."

"What's the matter with her?"

"I don't know. It's very bad. She's got a fever, and a headache, and a terrible cough, and her nose keeps running. She can't go nowhere."

"Now look here, Fran Ellen, I want you to give that note to your mother, and I want to see her. Is that clear?"

"Yes, ma'am."

"If she really is sick, she can come as soon as she feels better. You let her be the judge of that. You just take that note home and give it to her right away. Do you understand?"

"Yes, ma'am."

"It's not only that you have been leaving the school grounds during recess, and going I hate to

33

think where, but also I think your mother ought to know about the way you insult other children, continually pick fights, and . . . Fran Ellen Smith, take that finger out of your mouth, and don't stand so close to me!"

"Yes, ma'am."

I can't make up my mind what to do about that note. I think maybe I should show it to Fletcher, but then I think maybe he'll be so mad at me, he'll say I can't take care of Flora. So next day, I tell Miss Thompson that my mama will be in to see her soon as she feels better.

"Fine," says Miss Thompson. "I'll look forward to seeing her."

Every day she asks me how my mother is feeling, and I tell her pretty bad, no improvement. But I'm crazy thinking of ways to get home in the afternoons. I can't skip out during recess any more. I don't tell Florence what happened, but I ask her to run home at recess. She says No. She says Flora will be O.K.

Every day, I've got to think of a way to go home. Some days I say I have to go to the toilet, and run home real fast. Somedays I say I got to give the key to Florence, or I left my sweater in the yard at recess . . . or my books . . . or my homework. And somedays I just stay home and don't go to school at all.

I never have to worry about the Bears' House. It's always there when I come back.

Baby Bear is jumping up and down, and he's yelling, "I know something."

"Shut up your mouth," Mama Bear says, and gives him a little whack on his backside. Just a little, friendly whack because he keeps laughing and jumping and looking at me.

"Why is that door closed to the kitchen?" I ask Papa Bear.

"We're just waiting for Goldilocks," he says.

"Where is she?" I say.

Mama Bear opens that kitchen door just a crack and takes a quick look at something inside. She closes the door very carefully. "I just don't know where that girl goes off to," she says. "Sometimes she disappears for hours, and I hate to think where she goes."

"I'll talk to her, Mama Bear," I say.

"Well, maybe that would be best," she says. "She only listens to you."

Goldilocks comes in through the door. She is huffing and puffing from running so fast.

"Where you been, Goldilocks?" I ask her.

"In the toilet," she says. She is hiding something behind her back.

"Now don't give me none of that," I say. "You know there's no toilet in this house."

She looks like she's about to bust out crying, so quick I say, "Never mind, Goldilocks, and what's that you got behind your back?"

She kind of looks at Papa Bear sideways. I see he's shaking his head up and down at her, which means O.K. O.K. what? She brings her hand around in front of her. She is holding a big box wrapped in silver-and-gold paper and tied with the biggest red bow you ever saw. She holds out the box to me.

"What's this for?" I say.

Papa Bear opens the door to the kitchen. There is a tablecloth on the table, and all the fancy dishes and glasses are out. Every single one, and right in the center is the cake. With candles. Ten of them. Mama Bear baked it, and it is pink with red roses and green leaves. The kind of cake you see in bakery stores. Only bigger. And prettier. On top it says HAPPY BIRTHDAY, FRAN ELLEN, and there is a great big 10 in white frosting.

> Happy Birthday to you, (they all sing)
> Happy Birthday to you.
> Happy Birthday, dear Fran Ellen,
> Happy Birthday to you.

And everybody kisses me and hands me presents

with fancy paper and big bows. There are so many of them I have to pile them up on the floor.

The party lasts a long time. Miss Thompson has to go over the math for Philip Speevak, who was absent four days, so she doesn't tell me to go back to my seat until I am just about finished with my third helping of cake.

It was the best birthday I ever had. I'm glad I went to school that day.

MAY

"Not today, ma'am," I say. "She's running a high fever, and you're going to catch it if you come near her."

"Yes, *today*," Miss Thompson says. "I will go home with you after school, and we'll see just how sick your mother really is."

"Lady next door," I tell her, "came by the other day, and she's in the hospital now. She caught it real bad."

"Fran Ellen," teacher says, "stand over there, and wait for me. I don't believe a word you are saying."

"Yes, ma'am."

Teacher is busy opening and closing drawers in her desk, and jiggling all her papers. I move around to the Bears' House. Only Papa Bear is in the living room. He picks me up, and holds me tight in his

38

lap. Then he starts playing TROT, TROT TO BOSTON
with me.

> Trot, trot to Boston
> To buy a loaf of bread.
> Home again, home again
> The old horse is dead.

I don't want to go no place, but soon she's ready
to go.

Downstairs, she stops by her car, and says, "Do
you live far from the school?"

"Yes, ma'am," I say, even though it's right around
the corner. I don't get to ride in a car much.

She gets in the car, and opens the door for me.

"What street is it?" she says.

"Pierce, ma'am."

She starts the car, turns the corner, and we drive
along for a few blocks. I lean back in the seat, suck
my thumb, and try not to think about anything
unpleasant.

"What's the number, Fran Ellen?"

"Five-six-two, ma'am."

"Five-six-two? But we're on the nine-hundred
block. We must have passed the five hundreds."

"Yes, ma'am."

"Well, why didn't you tell me?" She does not
sound pleasant.

"I don't know, ma'am."

Miss Thompson turns the car around, and starts

back the other way. "If it's not too much trouble, Fran Ellen, will you please let me know when we arrive at your house!"

"Yes, ma'am."

She parks the car, and as we get out she says, "This is right around the corner from school, Fran Ellen. We didn't have to drive at all."

"Yes, ma'am."

"Then why in the world . . ." But she doesn't finish her question. We go up the stairs four flights, and every once in a while I go back to see if she's all right. She keeps stopping to lean against the bannister, but finally she makes it up.

"Just a minute," she says, breathing hard, and I watch her and see that she's an old lady, and not only a mean teacher.

As soon as we get inside, I hear Flora calling, "Fra Fra, Fra Fra!"

"That's me," I tell Miss Thompson. "She's calling me."

"I'm coming, baby," I yell, and I rush into the bedroom.

"Hup, Fra Fra," Flora says. I pick her up and kiss her, and there is Miss Thompson standing in the doorway, watching us.

"This here's my baby, Flora," I tell Miss Thompson. "She's not even ten months yet, but she says lots of things. She calls me Fra Fra, and she says

40

'hup' for up, and 'mook' for milk, and 'coo-coo' for Kool-Aid. Go ahead, Flora, say something to Miss Thompson," I tell her as I lay her down and begin changing her. "Say, 'Hi.' Go ahead. Say, 'Hi, Miss Thompson.'"

"Hi," says Flora. "Hi, coo-coo."

"That means, 'Hi,'" I say real fast, because maybe teacher will be insulted. "Flora means, 'Hi, I want my Kool-Aid.' Don't you, baby? Don't you, Flooziewoozie? Don't you, Franny's baby?"

"Well, look at that!" says Miss Thompson, coming closer and standing over the crib.

"Hi, coo-coo." Flora laughs, and wrinkles her nose and kicks her feet.

"Hey, hold still, you big silly," I say, but not in a mean voice, and I sprinkle powder on her bottom and put on a clean diaper.

"What a beautiful baby," says Miss Thompson. "She is . . . well, will you just look at that . . . what eyes! . . . and what a beautiful face."

"Hi, coo-coo."

"Hi, yourself, you little beauty," says Miss Thompson.

I sit her up in her crib and brush her hair and put a little yellow bow in one of her curls.

"Coo-coo," Flora shouts.

"She wants her bottle," I tell Miss Thompson. I

41

pick up Flora, go on into the kitchen and fix a bottle for her.

"Fran Ellen, I can't get over how handy you are," Miss Thompson says. "You must be quite a little helper for your mother."

"Yes, ma'am." I hand Flora her bottle, and Flora sticks it in her mouth and begins to make loud sucking noises.

"What is that she's drinking?" Miss Thompson says.

"Kool-Aid, Miss Thompson. It's lime flavor. That's green, but it's a pink bottle so that's why the color looks kind of funny."

"Kool-Aid is not very nutritious," teacher says. "I hope she drinks something else besides Kool-Aid."

"Yes, ma'am," I tell her, "she does. She drinks milk sometimes. At night, she likes a bottle of milk."

"Does your mother *know* you give the baby Kool-Aid?" Miss Thompson says, and she sounds like herself. "I have a feeling she may not approve your giving the baby Kool-Aid."

"Oh, it's fine with her, Miss Thompson. We're all crazy about Kool-Aid in my family. Maybe you'd like a cup. Would you like a cup of Kool-Aid, Miss Thompson?"

"No, thank you," says Miss Thompson. She stops looking at the baby, and you can just see her looking over the kitchen. "I would like to see your mother now, Fran Ellen."

I am just about to say I believe my mother is not at home. That maybe she went to the doctor. When we both hear the bedroom door open, and Mama passes by, maybe on her way to look in the mail-box.

"Mama," I say real loud, "here's Miss Thompson, my teacher, Mama. She came by to see you, Mama."

Miss Thompson clears her throat, and says, "How do you do, Mrs. Smith. I'm sorry to disturb you, but . . ."

Mama goes right on walking out of the apartment and down the stairs to the mailbox.

"She's expecting an important letter," I tell Miss Thompson. "With money in it."

"Oh!" she says.

"Why don't you sit down," I say, and lead her into the living room. I move some blankets off the sofa.

Miss Thompson sits down. We both wait. I am thinking of what to do. Flora stops sucking and holds out her bottle to Miss Thompson. "Hi, coo-coo," she says.

We all laugh, Flora the loudest.

"Would you like to hold her?" I say.

"I don't know if she'd come to me," says Miss

Thompson. "After all, she doesn't know me, and I think she'd be a little frightened."

"Not her," I say. I put Flora in Miss Thompson's lap, and Miss Thompson sits up very stiff and holds Flora very tight. Flora puts up one hand and tries to pull off Miss Thompson's glasses.

"No, baby," I say. "No, no, naughty!"

"Nutty?" Flora says. She puts her hand down and wrinkles up her face and laughs up at Miss Thompson.

"Oh, what a darling!" Miss Thompson says. "Yes," she says to Flora, "you are a darling! A precious, lovely, little darling!"

Flora begins to move her hand up toward Miss Thompson's glasses.

Then Mama and Fletcher come back into the room together. Mama keeps going toward the bedroom, but Fletcher just stops still—frozen—like they do it on TV.

"Fletcher," I say, and I know he's going to let me have it later, "Fletcher, Miss Thompson came by to see Mama today."

"How are you, Miss Thompson?" Fletcher says, and Mama goes right on into the bedroom. "I'm happy to see you."

"And I'm happy to see you, Fletcher," says Miss Thompson, and she really does look happy to see him. She was his teacher too in fourth grade. "How are you, Fletcher, and how do you like junior high school?"

"I like it very much, Miss Thompson," he says, looking friendly at her and mean at me at the same time.

"How are your marks?"

"Pretty good, ma'am. I was on the honor roll last report-card period."

Flora makes a pass at Miss Thompson's glasses, so I pick her up and carry her back to the bedroom.

"Naughty, naughty," I say, and kiss her nose.

She snuggles up to my neck, and it takes awhile before I get her settled in her crib. When I come back into the living room, Fletcher is sitting next to Miss Thompson and talking so fast he doesn't sound like him. He's talking about some book he just read, and he's all excited about something inside the book, and Miss Thompson's all excited listening, and neither one of them notices me.

Which is fine. Now that Fletcher is handling the situation, I won't have to worry so much. I guess I should have told him before. I sit down on a pile of underwear on the green chair, and get my thumb in the right spot, nice and warm and wet in my mouth.

Fletcher is telling Miss Thompson how he got in some class called an Honors English Class, and how the teacher didn't think he belonged there because he was so quiet and didn't speak up. One day when Fletcher handed in a book report about that book he was telling Miss Thompson about, the teacher didn't even believe he did it himself. But after awhile, when she had him do work in the classroom and saw it was really him, she changed and couldn't be nicer.

Fletcher laughs. He's not acting like he always acts around the house. He's quiet around the house. Miss Thompson laughs too, and she says, "Fletcher, I know you're going to do very well in school. You have a good attitude, and you're willing to work hard. The important thing, Fletcher, is to persevere, and not be discouraged. Always be polite and respectful to your teachers even if you don't always agree with them. Remember, Fletcher, your teachers are ready to help you, but you must want to learn . . ."

And so on. That's the way she talks. Me, I always stop listening, but Fletcher's lapping it all up, smiling and nodding, and saying, "Yes, I know. I think so too. I try, Miss Thompson, I really try."

I suck a little harder on my thumb, and after awhile, they stop talking and laughing. I know they're looking at me now.

"Well, Fletcher," says Miss Thompson, "I'm so happy I had a chance to talk to you. But I really must have a word or two with your mother. I wouldn't dream of bothering her. I know she's been ill. But I consider it very important, so would you please ask her to speak with me for a moment or two."

Fletcher's thinking hard. He goes off into the bedroom, and after a few minutes, Mama comes out, wearing a house dress over her nightgown.

"I'm sorry, Mrs. Smith," says Miss Thompson, "to disturb you when you're not feeling well, but I'm afraid we have a very serious problem on our hands with Fran Ellen, and before taking the matter to the principal, I thought—I hope—we might be able to work something out between us."

Mama just stands there, looking at Miss Thompson, and not looking at her.

"Mama?" Fletcher says.

"Yes?" Mama says politely.

"Why don't you sit down, Mama," says Fletcher. He helps her into the chair across the room from where Miss Thompson is sitting.

"You see, Mrs. Smith," says Miss Thompson, "Fran Ellen plays hooky from school. I'm sorry to use such a harsh word, but the situation has become very grave. For a while, she disappeared only during the afternoon recess, and I don't know where she went. Once she saw that I knew what she was up to, she began finding other ways to get out of school. Lately, there have been days when she just doesn't come to school at all. She brings me notes that I am quite sure you never wrote, saying she had a headache, or a cold or a sprained ankle. There are other problems too, Mrs. Smith, that you should know about. She picks on other children, calls them names, gets into fights. And then, there is—her appearance. This thumb sucking, Mrs. Smith, is ridiculous in a girl her age. It makes her look funny, and —yes—it makes her smell unpleasant too."

I take my finger out of my mouth, but not before Fletcher and Miss Thompson have looked me over with the same kind of look in their eyes.

"Mama?" says Fletcher.

"Yes?" Mama says politely to Miss Thompson.

"So that's why I'm here, Mrs. Smith. I knew you would want to know how serious a problem we are having with Fran Ellen, and I feel certain you will want to do something about it."

Fletcher says, "I'm sure my mother will see that none of this happens again. Right, Mama?"

Fletcher can always get Mama to give the right answer when the Welfare Lady comes. But today, Mama looks at Fletcher, and says, "Is there any mail today?"

"No, Mama," Fletcher says quickly. "You just looked yourself, and there wasn't any mail."

"No mail, no mail," Mama begins to cry. "Never any mail."

"Never mind, Mama," I say. "Maybe tomorrow there will be mail."

"That's right," says Fletcher. "Come on, Mama, lie down and take a rest. You'll feel better." He takes her hand, and she gets up and goes with him into the bedroom.

"I guess," I say to Miss Thompson, "I'm not going to suck my thumb no more."

"Fran Ellen," she kind of whispers to me, "your mother is sick."

"Yes, ma'am," I say. "I told you that already. And ma'am, I really am sorry I make so much trouble. I'll be good from now on."

"But Fran Ellen, you said she had a fever and a cough."

"Yes, ma'am, and I won't fight no more."

"Fra Fra! Hup, Fra Fra!" shouts Flora.

I go, and get her, and sit her on my lap. Miss Thompson is looking the place over, and I am waiting for Fletcher to come back and handle the situation. So I don't say anything else to Miss Thompson. I play TROT, TROT TO BOSTON with Flora. She practically laughs her head off. Finally Fletcher comes out of the bedroom, very slow.

Miss Thompson says to him, "I think I had better talk to your father."

I wait for Fletcher to say something, but he doesn't. So I say, "Yes, ma'am."

"When would be a good time to call him?" she says.

I don't know why, but cat's got Fletcher's tongue. "There's no phone," I say.

"He can call me then."

"He works late, ma'am." I look hard at Fletcher to make him wake up. He just keeps looking at the floor.

"Fletcher," says Miss Thompson, "I insist on speaking with your father. I know I can trust you. Now, when will your father be able to talk to me?"

> Trot, trot to Boston
> To buy a loaf of bread.
> Home again, home again
> The old horse is dead.

I sing, and let Flora drop between my legs. She just about cracks up laughing, but Fletcher doesn't say a word.

"Fletcher?" says Miss Thompson, and she is surprised. "I'm talking to you, Fletcher."

"Yes, ma'am," Fletcher finally says, but he keeps on looking at the floor.

That's not a good answer, because she starts looking the place over again. Then she looks at me and Flora. "Fran Ellen," she says, "where do you go when you run away from school?"

She's got a funny, smart look to her, and I know

she's getting hot. Fletcher won't be any good at all, I know for sure, so I begin crying, and whining like Florence. "Please, ma'am," I say, "I don't go no place special. Maybe just to the store for gum or candy, but no place special. And, ma'am, after this, I promise I'll never play hooky again."

She is still looking at me with that funny look. "Please," I yell, and I get my voice up in a squeal like Florence, "just don't tell my daddy. He'll give me a beating if you tell him, ma'am. Please, and you'll see, I'll be good and never suck my thumb again. Just don't tell my daddy."

Which gets her thinking about him instead of me.

"Yes," says Miss Thompson, "your father. I want to talk to your father."

I am crying my head off. "Tomorrow," I yell, "you want he should call you tomorrow? Please, ma'am, don't talk to him tomorrow."

"Tomorrow," she says, getting up. "I insist upon speaking to him tomorrow. Fletcher, I know I can't depend on Fran Ellen, so will you please ask your father to call me at this number?" She hands him a piece of paper.

"Please, teacher, please!" I yell, "just don't tell my daddy. He'll be so mad if you tell him. Honest, I promise to be good. I won't give you no more trouble."

"No, Fran Ellen, I'm afraid I will have to speak with your father."

She starts giving me all the reasons why, but at least she isn't looking at me with that funny, smart look. After awhile, she goes. Then I really give it to Fletcher. After I finish with him, he starts on me.

"And what's going to happen tomorrow?" he says. "Why did you say Daddy would call her tomorrow? You know he's not going to call her tomorrow."

"I had to get her out of here before she found out, didn't I? She was getting pretty hot, and you didn't do anything."

"So now what are we going to do tomorrow?"

"I tell you what we're going to do tomorrow. Only it's what you're going to do, because she trusts you. You're going to call her tomorrow, and tell her somebody died—say Granddaddy, because he's already dead so it won't hurt him none—and Daddy had to go home for the funeral. Say we got somebody, make up a somebody, say your aunt Marcie, looking after us while he's gone. Say he's got to stay awhile to look after things, but you'll have him call soon as he gets back."

Fletcher says No. He says he is scared. Funny— he can lie to all sorts of grownups, so why should Miss Thompson make him scared. I am scared too. Not of her, but of what would happen if she finds

out and tells. And if they come for us and take away
my Flora.

Fletcher is scared. But I know something that will
scare him even more.

So I tell him, "Listen, Fletcher, if you don't do it,
they will come and take Mama away."

Fletcher says O.K., he will do it. Next day I go
down to the drug store with him. I sit in the phone
booth with him while he calls. He sounds phony to
me, but she believes him.

Later, when we get home, he really tears into me
for getting us into all this mess. But I don't mind.
Flora is safe.

JUNE

Almost every day for a while she keeps on asking how things are at home. Did my daddy get back yet? How was my mama feeling? And what about my aunt Marcie? Was she staying with us?

"No, ma'am," I'd say, "he's planning to come back in a couple weeks or so. His mama, my grandma's not feeling so well, and she'd like for him to stay."

And "Oh, yes, ma'am, my mama's much better. She's up and out of bed now." And "Aunt Marcie's going to stay until Daddy gets back. She's been looking after Mama and Flora, and baking us all pie."

After awhile she forgets to ask. But I have to be very careful. First of all, I don't suck my thumb any more. I just holler, "Who you hitting?" when they pile on me. But like I promised her, I don't suck my thumb. Nobody notices I don't suck my

54

thumb any more. Even Miss Thompson doesn't notice right away. I notice it all the time. My thumb has no place to go. It hurts so much. I hold it in my other hand sometimes, and rock it, and tell it never mind, we got Flora. But it still hurts, and my mouth doesn't hang natural, and some days I don't think I can keep the two of them away from each other.

It hurts so. But the kids still say, "Thumb Sucker" and go "Yuk!" like I smell.

"Go ahead, Thumb Sucker," Jennifer says. "Call Susan a dope. She won't mind."

"Uh, uh," I say, and hold my thumb tight so it won't hurt so much.

Jennifer comes closer, holds her nose, and says, "Go ahead, Fran Ellen. You'll really like it this time because, honest, she won't mind. Right, Susan?"

"Right," says Susan.

So finally I call Susan a dope, and Susan smacks me. I yell, "Who you hitting?" and Jennifer smacks me. Then, this one time, my hand, the one that has the thumb, reaches out and gives Jennifer a real hard one, right on her nose. So she starts yelling. They all start yelling, and Miss Thompson runs over and pulls me off.

"Now what?" she says. "Not only do you insult Susan, but what reason did you have to hit Jennifer?"

"I'm not sucking my thumb, ma'am," I tell her.

"You're not sucking your thumb?" She thinks about that. "Why, that's right. You're not."

"Because I told you I wouldn't," I say.

"Well, that's fine. I'm very pleased." She looks like she might even smile. Then she hears Jennifer bawling, and says, "But that's no reason to hit Jennifer, is it?"

"Yes, ma'am," I tell her. "I've got nothing else to do with it."

Maybe I wasn't so careful that time, but after that Jennifer and Susan don't play the game so much. Maybe it's also because teacher's watching me a lot more than she used to, and they don't want to take the chance. They still step on my feet and push me in the stomach and bump into me, but they don't play the game.

So after a couple of weeks, Miss Thompson says, "I'm glad to see, Fran Ellen, that you've learned to control yourself in so many ways. You look one hundred per cent better without your thumb in your mouth, and I am even more pleased to see that you've stopped picking on Susan and Jennifer and have been keeping out of fights. And then you haven't been playing hooky. I think you are beginning to understand that good habits are necessary to achieve . . ."

And so on. I don't listen to what she keeps on

saying, but I guess she will forget about talking to my father. But I keep on being careful.

I don't run home during school anymore. Fletcher said I had to stop. I didn't like it, and neither did Flora, but I knew he was right. Fletcher said he, Felice and Florence would have to look after Flora in the afternoon, but no cutting out of school. They would just have to take turns staying out for a day or two at a time.

Florence didn't mind, but Felice did. Everytime it was her turn to stay home she cried, and one day when I got home from school, Flora was yelling her head off, and there were three big pinch marks on her little arm, all turning blue. Now, only Florence and Fletcher take turns. Fletcher failed a test and missed going to the science museum when his class went on their outing, and he didn't eat his supper that night even though it was canned ravioli.

"Never mind," I told him. "It will be summer soon, and everything will be easier."

I know it will be easier in the summer. Flora will be happier then, because I will be taking care of her all the time. She is not happy now. She stands up and rocks in her crib and tries to get out. She's not taking so many naps any more, and she cries and cries sometimes even when somebody is playing with her. Sometimes even when it's me. There is a rash on her stomach and back that does not go away. Maybe that's why she cries so much. We keep putting powder on it, but it doesn't help.

Fletcher says she needs to see a doctor. He says babies are supposed to have all sorts of shots which she never had. But a grownup is supposed to take a baby to the doctor, not a sister or brother. Fletcher is worried. He is worried because maybe Flora is getting sick, and he is worried because if we take her to the doctor, somebody will find out about us.

I am worried too. Every morning now when I leave to go to school, I can hear Flora crying. I have to stick my fingers in my ears, and sing real loud or I won't be able to go. And Fletcher says I have to go. And when I'm in school, I have to be careful not to look worried. I keep telling myself, another couple weeks and school's out. Then it will be summer.

Summer. No more school. No more Miss Thompson. No more Bears' House.

I got to prepare them for what's coming.

"Even if you don't like it," I tell Goldilocks, "you've got to persevere. If you want to amount to anything you've got to get along with others . . ."

She's not listening. She says, "Are you coming too?"

I'm busy ironing out a wrinkle in my yellow-and-

58

red dress with the iron in Mama Bear's kitchen. It's a black iron, really made of iron. You don't plug it in the way irons work today. You heat it up on the stove.

"Well," I tell her, "I might have to go away on a business trip."

"If you don't go, I don't go," says Goldilocks. She starts crying, and hollering, and Mama Bear comes running in.

"Now what?" she says.

"Fran Ellen says she's not coming with us this summer."

Mama Bear puts her hands on her hips, and says, "How come?"

"Well, you see, Mama Bear, there's these two girls, Jennifer James and Rosalie Gonzales. Rosalie's a big show-off, but she's not so bad, but I think Jennifer . . ."

"I hate Jennifer," says Mama Bear. "We'll just go on the way we are."

"I'd like that fine," I tell her, "but I'm afraid it's not going to work out. I can't do anything about it either."

"Well, you just better do something," she says, "because nobody's taking you away from us, and nobody's taking us from you, and I'm not going to stand for it!"

Then she hollers for Papa Bear, and he makes a

big fuss about how he's not going to stand for it, and Baby Bear screams his head off.

It's not going to be easy. I can't figure out what to do. I think maybe if I could get my thumb in my mouth I'd be able to work something out.

Last day of school, I hang up my sweater in the closet, and stop by on my way back to my seat.

"'Bye," I say to them.

All of them start to yell.

"Don't forget to lock up," I tell them, and then I get away fast because I'm crying too, and I got to stop before somebody sees.

Jennifer's wearing a white dress with big yellow flowers. She's got yellow shoes, and she is the prettiest girl I ever saw, except for Flora. I forget she is Jennifer, and say to her, "That sure is a pretty dress."

She says, "Yuk!"

Rosalie Gonzales has the most stars next to her name for reading, spelling, social, math and science. Only in P.E. she doesn't have more stars than anybody else. Maybe Miss Thompson will give her the Bears' House. The McFarlane twins say she will give it to Rosalie because didn't she say the child who tried the hardest will earn it. They say Rosalie tried the hardest to get the best marks, and that's true. But Jennifer tried the hardest to make teacher like her the best. I think it will be Jennifer.

I am wrong. The McFarlane twins are wrong too.
Miss Thompson gives the Bears' House to me.

"How come?" Jennifer screams. "How come her?
What she do?"

"She's the worst kid in the class," Rosalie says.
"She's bad and dumb and dirty."

Everybody's yelling. Nobody's happy.

Teacher begins to talk about how she said she
was going to give it to the child who worked the
hardest, and that she thinks I worked the hardest.
She tells them about how I stopped fighting,
stopped sucking my thumb, and stopped playing
hooky from school, and that these were great things
for somebody like me. She says how not everybody
is the same, and how what's easy for one person is
twice as hard for somebody else. And that maybe
I wasn't the smartest, but I tried, and the important
thing she says is for a person to try, to persevere, and
to demonstrate a willingness . . .

And so on. Lots of people are arguing, and teacher
keeps talking and talking and talking. I got no time
to listen. Soon as she says my name, I don't even
wait to be surprised. I get myself over to my Bears'
House and start packing.

"It's all right," I tell Goldilocks, and put her in my
pocket.

"Don't worry about a thing," I tell Mama Bear,
and put her next to Goldilocks.

The Bears' House

But I am worried: How I'm going to get home without them piling on me, I don't know. But I'm going to do it!

"Fran Ellen," Miss Thompson says, "what are you doing?"

"I'm getting ready to take the Bears' House, ma'am."

"Well, you can't manage yourself. Who will volunteer to help Fran Ellen take the Bears' House home?"

Nobody does, and they all start yelling all over again. "It's not fair." "She's a dirty Thumb Sucker." "Teacher's a cheater."

"Fran Ellen," says Miss Thompson, "I will help you take the Bears' House home."

A couple of them kick me and punch me. Susan says she will be around looking for me, but I don't expect she will find me. I will be inside my house the whole summer.

Teacher puts everything in her car and drives me around the corner. She helps me carry the Bears' House and the furniture and the dolls up the stairs. I keep telling her not to bother, but she says she wants to.

Outside the door, I say "Thank you," but she says she will help me carry everything inside. Fletcher opens the door. He is carrying Flora, and the rash is all over her face now.

"Well, hello, Fletcher," says Miss Thompson. "You're home early from school, aren't you?"

"Yes ma'am," Fletcher says.

"But look at the baby!" Miss Thompson kind of yells. "What a horrible rash. What's wrong with her?"

"It's the heat," I say, "and thank you very much, ma'am, for helping me bring the Bears' House home."

Fletcher says, "Excuse me." He carries Flora back in the bedroom, and closes the door.

We put the Bears' House down in the middle of the living room floor, and I take all the furniture from her.

"Thank you, Miss Thompson," I say. "I can manage fine now. I sure appreciate your giving me the Bears' House."

Flora begins to cry. You can hear her even though the door is closed.

Miss Thompson says, "Fran Ellen, is your father back yet?"

"No, ma'am," I say, "but we got a letter from him saying next week he . . ."

"Fran Ellen," she says, and there is that funny, smart look on her face, "where is your aunt Marcie?"

"Oh, she's out shopping, Miss Thompson."

Miss Thompson sits down. "I'll wait until she comes back," she says.

"She's going to be gone all day, ma'am. She went downtown, and we don't expect her back until very late."

The baby is screaming now, and you can hear Fletcher's feet going back and forth across the room.

Miss Thompson stands up, and heads for the door. I can't think of nothing else to do, so I run after her. I hold onto her arm, and I say, "Please, ma'am. Don't! Give us a break. We can manage."

"No, Fran Ellen," she says, "you can't manage. You are only children, and somebody should be looking after you." She takes away my hand from her arm, and she pats my shoulder, and looks in my face. "You poor thing," she says, "what a terrible time you must have had. But don't worry any more. I will handle everything." She goes out of the door.

And I know just how she will handle everything. She will tell. She will call the police, and soon they will be coming for us. To take us away. Like Fletcher said, they will take us to foster homes, and put Mama in a hospital for crazy people.

I run into the bedroom. Fletcher has put Flora back in her crib. She is screaming her head off, but she won't let me pick her up. I try to give her a

64

bottle of Kool-Aid, but she throws the bottle out of the crib.

Fletcher and I go out of the room and close the door. Maybe Flora will go to sleep and feel better. Fletcher says he is going down to do some shopping. There is no food in the house. He doesn't notice the Bears' House, and he forgets to say anything about Miss Thompson. So I don't tell him. He will find out soon enough.

After awhile Flora stops crying. I look in the room. She is asleep. I think maybe I will pack a few things and run away with her. Just me and Flora. I stand over the crib, and look at her, my baby, my beautiful Flora. Only she doesn't look beautiful now. The rash is over her eyelids now, and there is yellow gook on her eyelashes. I don't know what to do.

I come back to the living room, and look at my Bears' House on the floor. For the first time I am all alone with them. But my thumb is hurting so. I think now I can suck it. Why shouldn't I? So what if she did give me the Bears' House? It was mine, anyways, wasn't it?

But first I have to make them comfortable. I start fixing the furniture. I get it all in, and put them all in the living room. I put the welcome mat in front of the house. Then I go in.

Mama Bear is kissing Goldilocks. "I am really proud of you," she says.

Then Papa Bear kisses Goldilocks, and he says, "I am proud of you too."

"Me too," says Baby Bear.

"You kept your promise," Mama Bear says. "You said you weren't going to suck your thumb anymore, and you didn't."

"You persevered," says Papa Bear.

Goldilocks' face is one big smile.

"We're going to have a celebration," says Mama Bear. "I'm going to fix chicken and dumplings and pie. Come on, Goldilocks, let's get cooking."

"Won't be no fun," says Baby Bear, "unless Fran Ellen comes."

"I'm coming," I say.

They don't hear me. "She said she has to go away on a business trip," Goldilocks says, and she stops smiling.

"Hey, you dodos," I say, "I'm right here. Don't you hear?"

"She's taking the baby with her."

Mama Bear snorts. "Not Fran Ellen. She's not taking no baby with her. She's one smart girl, and she knows a baby has to be looked after proper. A baby has to be someplace where she gets good food and milk, and has a doctor taking care of her and making her rash go away. You think Fran Ellen wants to kill that baby? Why, she loves that baby best in the world! So don't talk such foolishness. Come on now, Goldilocks, let's go!"

They go out of the living room. Baby Bear goes along too. Papa Bear sits down in the rocking chair. He sees me standing in the doorway. "You came back?" he says.

"I never went away," I tell him.

"You gave us a scare," he says, and he holds out his arms to me.

"But Papa Bear," I say, "how do I know you won't go away or Mama Bear or Baby Bear or even Goldilocks?"

"We can't go away," he says. "This is your house, isn't it? So we will just be staying here for as long as you like."

"For sure?"

"For sure."

So then I sit in his lap, and he sings TROT, TROT TO BOSTON, and I lean against his shoulder, and I persevere, and I do not suck my thumb.

About the Author

MARILYN SACHS says, "When I was eight, my mother was in a terrible accident and spent nearly a year in the hospital. Nothing was right that year except for one thing. A kind, sympathetic teacher gave me a doll's house. It saved my life that year, and I never forgot it.

"When I grew up and became a writer, I tried to tell the story the way it had happened to me. But it didn't work. Over the years I tried to tell it in different ways, until I finally wrote *The Bears' House*. Fran Ellen's family and circumstances were very different from mine, but her joy over her Bears' House comes very close to the joy I felt over mine."

Marilyn Sachs is the author of many highly acclaimed books for children, including *Class Pictures*, *The Fat Girl*, and *Baby Sister*. *The Bears' House*, now in a new edition, was a National Book Award nominee, a *New York Times* Outstanding Book of the Year, and a *School Library Journal* Best Book of the Year.

Mrs. Sachs lives in San Francisco, California.